For L and G
"Fly high"
– H.F.

First published by Parragon in 2013

Parragon
Chartist House
15–17 Trim Street
Bath BA1 1HA, UK
www.parragon.com

Written by Margaret Wise Brown
Illustrated by Henry Fisher

Edited by Laura Baker
Designed by Ailsa Cullen
Production by Rob Simenton

ISBN 978-1-4723-0790-3

Printed in China

Away
in my Airplane

PaRragon
Bath • New York • Singapore • Hong Kong • Cologne • Delhi
Melbourne • Amsterdam • Johannesburg • Shenzhen

Riding along in my

airplane,

Over the clouds

and through the rain.

Riding along
in my airplane,

Sometimes I meet a bird
way up high in the sky,

Flying almost as fast as I fly—

But not as high!

Then out of the clouds

and sun again,

Riding along in my airplane!

Down below the people go, very small and very slow.

They look like bugs and ants and flies—
I wonder if they realize
What they look like to my eyes.

Riding along in my airplane,

I dash straight up in the air
And wheel about.

I plunge through the sunlight,

Then I glide

down to the earth

in my airplane.